my super-spy diary

THIS DIARY BELONGS TO

Eliza Boom

Eliza Boom

my super-spy diary

BY Emily Gale

ILLUSTRATED BY Joëlle Dreidemy

Aladdin * NEW YORK LONDON TORONTO SYDNEY NEW DELHI

With special thanks to
Justine Smith and Hannah Cohen

This book is a work of fiction. Any references to historical events, real people, or
real places are used fictitiously. Other names, characters, places, and events are products
of the author's imagination, and any resemblance to actual events or places
or persons, living or dead, is entirely coincidental.

ALADDIN

An imprint of Simon & Schuster Children's Publishing Division
1230 Avenue of the Americas, New York, NY 10020
First Aladdin paperback edition November 2014
Text copyright © 2014 by Emily Gale
Interior illustrations copyright © 2014 by Buster Books
Originally published in 2014 in Great Britain by Buster Books
Cover illustrations copyright © 2014 by Joëlle Dreidemy
Also available in an Aladdin hardcover edition.
All rights reserved, including the right of reproduction in whole or in part in any form.
ALADDIN is a trademark of Simon & Schuster, Inc., and related logo
is a registered trademark of Simon & Schuster, Inc.
For information about special discounts for bulk purchases, please contact
Simon & Schuster Special Sales at 1-866-506-1949 or business@simonandschuster.com.
The Simon & Schuster Speakers Bureau can bring authors to your live event. For more information
or to book an event contact the Simon & Schuster Speakers Bureau at 1-866-248-3049 or visit
our website at www.simonspeakers.com.
Cover design by Karin Paprocki
The text of this book was set in Brandon Grotesque.
Manufactured in the United States of America 1214 OFF
2 4 6 8 10 9 7 5 3
Library of Congress Control Number 2013956109
ISBN 978-1-4814-0653-6 (hc)
ISBN 978-1-4814-0652-9 (pbk)
ISBN 978-1-4814-0654-3 (eBook)

Monday Morning

My Lab, 7 a.m.

Dear Edison,

EMERGENCY!

I've lost my guinea pig. I know what you'll say:

You don't have a guinea pig, Eliza.

**My diary, named Edison
(after the famous scientist)**

Let me explain. It all has to do with my

new invention.

**That's me,
Eliza.**

Lately I've discovered that I can invent
POTIONS as well as GADGETS.

2

My first potion was for my best friend, Amy.

She desperately needed my help.

Amy's mom had washed her hair in mayonnaise after reading on the Internet that it kills lice.

Amy wants to smell like a GIRL . . .

. . . not an EGG!

Result: STINKY!

So I decided to create Egg-Away Shampoo (Potion No. 1) for Amy.

I thought about what girls smell like . . .

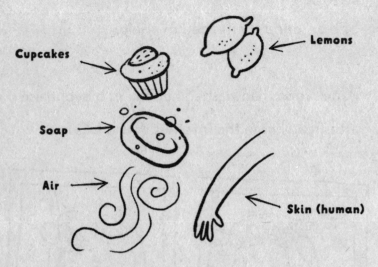

Cupcakes

Lemons

Soap

Air

Skin (human)

. . . and used all those things in my potion.

Potion No. 1:
Egg-Away
Shampoo

(Sometimes I smell of dog hair too, but I decided not to put any in the potion!)

Finally, we were ready for testing.

Step 1: Saturate test material (wet Amy's hair).

Step 2: Apply substance (rub in the shampoo).

Step 3: Flush excess substance (rinse it all off).

Step 4: Dehydrate test material (dry Amy's hair).

Result: FANTASTIC!

Then I discovered that someone else had a smelly problem.

Alice, my stepmom, was complaining nonstop about Einstein's stink. She's got a nose for trouble. Probably because she's a spy and strange smells are SUSPICIOUS.

Although Dad's a brilliant inventor, he's much too busy to make doggy shampoo. So it was up to me to save the day, and our noses.

Alice, a.k.a. Senior Agent Electra

Plum, baby spy who has potential

Dad, Chief Inventor

Einstein, my furry sidekick

Me, Junior Spy AND Assistant Inventor!!

MY FAMILY

Einstein and I got to work in my lab. First we needed thinking time. I put on some music to help us relax—I always have my best ideas when I'm relaxed.

THE MUSIC WORKED! I knew exactly what should go into the potion. Since Einstein is one of the family, he should smell like all of us!

Potion No. 2: Poochie-Pooh Solution

Ingredients:

1. My toothpaste

2. Dad's shaving cream

3. Plum's diaper-rash cream (only smells nice in the tube, not on her bottom)

4. Alice's face cream

The mixture was a bit stiff, so I added some lemonade. Fizz!

It was time for testing. But first I had to ask Einstein a very important question.

Will you be my guinea pig?

Not a REAL guinea pig, of course! Guinea pig is the name you give to someone you're testing an invention on.

I decided to be a guinea pig too. It was only fair.

I knew Poochie-Pooh was going to be fantastic . . . it felt lovely and fizzy on my head. FIZZ-TASTIC!

The trouble started when we got to "Step 3: Flush excess substance." Einstein HATES lots of water.

So that's how I lost my guinea pig. And now I REALLY NEED to find him.

Yours with fizz-tastic hair,

Eliza Boom

Junior Potions Master

Monday Afternoon
Our Garden, 4 p.m.

Dear Edison,

I have made a discovery. There's a new neighbor next door, and I have PROOF that she is mean and horrible.

PROFILE: lady next door
FIRST IMPRESSIONS:
mean, angry
PROBABLY LOOKS LIKE: →

Here's what happened. I followed Einstein's sticky paw prints all around the garden.

While I was hunting for Einstein in the garden, I heard a lady's voice on the other side of the fence.

And I saw Einstein squeeze underneath. He looked terrified!

When I tried to get him back inside the house
using a genius scientific method . . .

. . . he didn't even lick his lips! Our new

neighbor had been so horrible she'd made him

lose his appetite. Why did she shoo him away?

It was a new MYSTERY and I was going

to SOLVE IT!

It was a good opportunity to try out one of my latest inventions, the Super-Legs. I used them to peek over the fence.

My Super-Legs Invention:

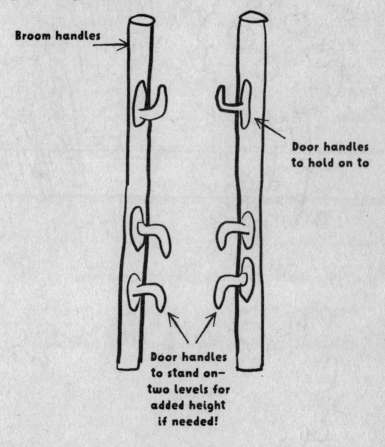

Broom handles

Door handles to hold on to

Door handles to stand on— two levels for added height if needed!

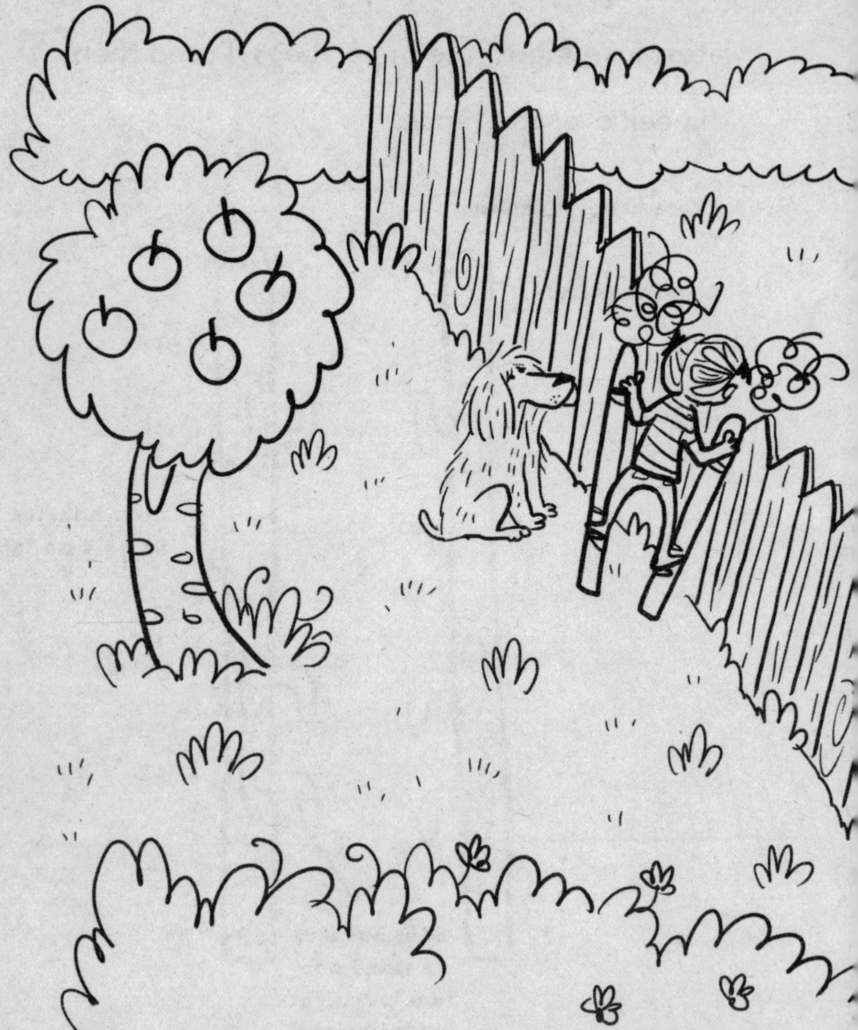

I couldn't see the lady, but I could see a BEAUTIFUL DOG. That's when I realized what was wrong with Einstein.

He'd found a friend, and our horrible neighbor was trying to keep them apart. If anyone tried to keep me away from Amy, I'd be upset too.

AAAAMYYY

ELIIIZAAA

Einstein was so heartbroken he chewed right through one of my Super-Legs!
Yours hopping-mad,
Eliza Boom
Living next door to an official baddie

Monday Evening
Kitchen Table, 6 p.m.

Dear Edison,

Things just got really weird. The doorbell
rang and it was a lady. Not just ANY lady, but
THE HORRIBLE LADY FROM NEXT DOOR.

Two things were SUSPICIOUS:
1. She didn't look horrible.
2. She had muffins. And they
   didn't look horrible either. They
   looked . . . DELICIOUS.

SUSPICIOUS vs. DELICIOUS.

I was confused, Edison.

19

First she introduced herself.

Hello, I'm Mrs. McNice.

Then she introduced her muffins.

Hello, we are special dairy-free muffins.

↑

The muffins didn't really speak . . . now, THAT would be an interesting invention!

Dairy-free, Edison! How could she know I am totally allergic to dairy?

Mrs. McNice stayed and chatted for a while.
When she went to use the bathroom, everyone
talked about how lovely she seemed.

I decided not to tell anyone that I'd thought
Mrs. McNice was HORRIBLE before. After all,
I've got my reputation as a Junior Spy to protect.

Before she left, I asked Mrs. McNice about her beautiful dog.

That's my Nancy. She's terribly shy. I'm so sorry I had to ask your lovely doggy to leave my garden. Nancy was scared of him.

And that's when I had to admit it, Edison.

I had been COMPLETELY WRONG about Mrs. McNice.
Yours guiltily,
Eliza Boom
Awesome Junior Spy
99% of the time

Guilty eyes

Monday Night
My Lab, 8 p.m.

Dear Edison,

The Boom household is very STRESSED OUT. None of us has had any sleep. It all started after I finally convinced Einstein to let me rinse off the Poochie-Pooh Solution.

In return I promised to get him closer to Nancy.

Einstein was whimpering under the hose. He hates water like I hate swimming. And I've got a swimming lesson tomorrow. Argh!

What no one seems to realize is . . .

. . . SWIMMING IS SUSPICIOUS.

WHY SWIMMING IS SUSPICIOUS:

1. a) Fingers before swimming . . . $\longrightarrow$

Before: smooth

b) Fingers after swimming.

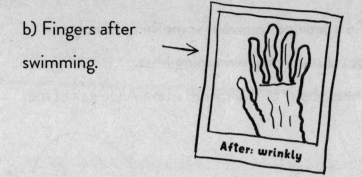

After: wrinkly

2. The drains at the bottom of the pool! Where do they go? And what lives in them?

Swimming pool drain monster

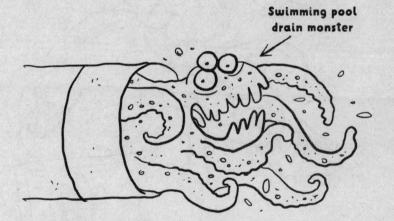

3. Can anyone REALLY be sure that swimming pool water isn't leaking into MY PRECIOUS BRAIN?

So I decided to invent something to help me
get through my swimming lesson ALIVE.
I was about to start work when Alice called me.

I was super excited—maybe she had a new spy
job for us!

But it wasn't a spy job at all.

It was a Plum job.

Her night light was nowhere to be seen.

Plum can't sleep without
her night light.

Plum's
night light

Alice was in despair. And all eyes were on
Einstein. Even mine. He has a habit of burying
things in secret stashes—often under the bed
or in the garden.

But spying on Einstein to see where he'd
hidden the night light would have to wait. First
I had to use music to get Plum to sleep . . .

Plum's room

. . . so I could stay in my lab and keep working on my swimming lesson invention. My lesson was in less than eleven hours. Argh!

My room

Yours inventively,

Eliza Boom

Super-Spy/Super-Bad Swimmer

Tuesday Morning
The Bathroom, 8 a.m.

Dear Edison,

My swimming lesson is in one hour.

Scared eyes

But I've decided to face my fears . . . with lots of safety equipment.

My new Learn-Away Swim-a-Fish invention is brilliant, even if I do say so myself.

The Learn-Away Swim-a-Fish:

Plum's baby-food bowls fixed to my hair band (to cover my ears)

Snorkel

Swimming floats

Dad said something last night that he hoped might make me feel better.

Eliza, as soon as you learn to swim, you'll be just like a fish.

But I think he got that backward.

AS SOON AS I'M LIKE A FISH, I'LL LEARN TO SWIM.

So I need to glide through the water like a fish, breathe underwater like a fish, and have hidden ears . . . like a fish!

Me, in fish form, swimming perfectly

Alice has just finished a bubble bath, so now I can use the water for testing my invention.

Stand back, Edison—

I'm going in!

Tuesday Morning
Our Car, 8:45 a.m.

Dear Edison,

We're buckled up in the car and ready to head to the pool.

Testing went as well as it could. It's not easy to swim in a bath, and I couldn't see because of all the bubbles.

I've just seen Mrs. McNice carrying FOUR HUGE PLANKS OF WOOD.

What would she be doing with those?

Hang on, I'm going to ask Alice if this is SUSPICIOUS.

Suspicious eyes

Oh well, Alice says it is NOT suspicious.

I asked her if she was sure. She said
DEFINITELY.

I asked her again. She said ABSOLUTELY.

I asked her again. She said

ELIZA!
PLEASE!

We're moving now, Edison. I'd better stop

because I can hardly read my writing!

Tuesday Afternoon
My Lab, 3 p.m.

Dear Edison,

I know you want to know how my swimming
lesson went.

But I don't want to talk about it. EVER.

So I'll draw it.

1.

**Zoe Wakefield—
Class Meanie/Mean Amphibian
(i.e., mean on land
AND water)**

2.

3.

4.

I knew swimming was SUSPICIOUS!

That's loads of suspicious things! I decided to make a Suspicious List:

THINGS I FIND SUSPICIOUS:

1. Zoe Wakefield (why so mean?)

2. Yogurt (smells like trouble)

3. Mrs. McNice (shouty one minute, brings muffins the next . . . and why does she need those huge planks of wood??!)

4. Swimming (how other kids can do it is a MYSTERY)

I don't have time to mope around. I need to hunt down where Einstein has buried Plum's night light. But I'm going to need an invention. . . .

I've got an idea! This time, I've been inspired by bats because they are such great HUNTERS.

Check out my new Echo-Detector invention:

A headlamp: bats have amazing eyesight in the dark.

A kazoo: bats make noise to help them find their prey.

Big ears made out of papier-mâché painted black: bats have super hearing.

Wings made out of black trash bags: wings just for decoration (but I wish I could fly!).

Bats use sound to hunt down their prey.

So I'm going to use sound to find Einstein's
secret stash of all the things he has stolen.

Einstein is giving me a strange look. Probably
feeling guilty.

Strange,
guilty eyes

Yours in mission-mode,

Eliza Boom

a.k.a. Bat-Girl, off to hunt down

Einstein's stash

Tuesday Night
My Lab, 8 p.m.

Dear Edison,

Things did not go as expected.

Being a bat is harder than it looks. I hunted like a bat all over the garden and found . . .

. . . NOTHING!

When I stopped, however, I DID hear a
SUSPICIOUS NOISE.

It was coming from Mrs. McNice's house.

First the ENORMOUS planks of wood,
and now a strange FIZZY-BUZZY sound.
What could be going on in there? Edison,
is it possible I was right? Is Mrs. McNice
SUSPICIOUS after all?

Friendly   Suspicious

I really need Alice to train me properly on how to be a good spy, but she's too busy trying to get Plum to sleep without the night light. It's getting late. I'll have to decide about Mrs. McNice tomorrow.

Night-night, don't let the bats bite.

Yours suspiciously,

Eliza Boom

Assistant Inventor Junior Spy, who will never swim like a fish, or hunt like a bat, ever!

Wednesday Morning
Our Garden, 11 a.m.

Dear Edison,

I'm at my new outdoor lab (it's also the garden bench). Amy's here too. She's come to help me.

Earlier, Dad was locked in his shed and Alice was in her spy bunker underneath the garden, busy doing top secret things.

So we were in charge of Plum.

I had thought of a way to spy on Mrs. McNice

AND get Einstein closer to Nancy . . .

ANOTHER POTION!

My plan was to
cover Einstein in a
perfume that would
make him irresistible
to lady dogs.

Then we'd go to Mrs. McNice's house. While the dogs got to know each other, I'd find out what that strange fizzy-buzzy noise was.

Some possible explanations for the FIZZY-BUZZY sound are:

1. Indoor beehive

2. Large collection of snakes

BUZZ

HZZZ

FIZZ

3. Lemonade maker

Potion No. 3: Lovey-Dovey-Doggy $\longrightarrow$

was easy to make.

Plum picked petals from the
rosebush that grows on top of our
secret spy bunker.

We mixed petals with sugar and seltzer water.
Alice says seltzer water is for special occasions
and this was one of those: Einstein's feelings for
Nancy are REAL.

We dabbed the potion behind Einstein's ears and did a sniff test.

He needed a bit more . . . and a bit more . . .

Result:
He looked like a wet
rosebush. But he
smelled great!

Unfortunately, Plum started playing copycat . . .
or rather, copydog and . . .

. . . splashed the potion everywhere. Poor Einstein got soaked and ran away again!

Where could he be? Is he with Nancy at Mrs. McNice's house? This calls for a new spy invention. Amy had to go, but now I'm back in my lab, Edison, making my next invention.
Yours stickily,
Eliza Boom
Inventor, Spy (and missing her furry sidekick)

Wednesday Night
My Lab, 8 p.m.

Dear Edison,

Meet my new invention: The Magni-Goggles.

← Magnifying glasses taped to top of goggles. Pull down over goggles for x 1,000 extra magnification—for super hands-free spying!

It is very reliable, UNLIKE the rest of today, which was very SUSPICIOUS.

With the Magni-Goggles in place, I crept along to Plum's bedroom window to get a good view of Mrs. McNice's living room. I had to see if Einstein was there.

But when I took my first peek, this is what
I saw:

Mrs. McNice looking right back at me!

When I found the courage to look again, she'd vanished.

I stayed watching for ages with my spy notepad . . .

Here's what my pad looked like after two hours:

2 p.m. No movement

2:30 p.m. Still nothing

3 p.m. Fly lands on windowsill

3:05 p.m. Fly flies away

4 p.m. I miss that fly

And then came the most difficult test of my spy abilities. . . .

I could smell baking! The smell was so good that real tears came into my eyes.

Hungry eyes

But I couldn't possibly move! Spies cannot just leave their position. It's the first rule of a stakeout.

At last, there was something to look at.

I saw Alice and Plum, with a tray of cupcakes
(that's what I could smell!), walking up
Mrs. McNice's front path.

Was Alice giving Mrs. McNice cupcakes
just to be nice? OR had she become
SUSPICIOUS about her like me?

We needed a family spy meeting ASAP.

Just then Einstein came running in, howling.

HE WAS COVERED IN ANTS!

Poor thing. Instead of making Nancy fall in love with him, I'd made ants fall in love with the sticky potion that was all over his fur!

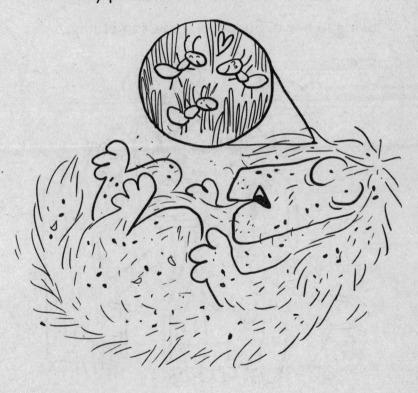

With only one Super-Leg left, I had to use the boring old bench to spy over the fence again. What was going on in there with Mrs. McNice and Alice and Plum and the cupcakes?

I hosed off Einstein at the same time. He was being so brave. Suddenly, I saw something strange.

I spied Nancy, the lady dog, sitting beside a table. HERE IS THE SUSPICIOUS PART...

... Nancy was right next to the cupcakes but she wasn't even sniffing them! If Einstein saw those cupcakes, this is what would happen:

Before   **After**

I ran to get my Magni-Goggles for a better look out of Plum's bedroom window.

When Alice got home, she asked me why she could see me spying on Mrs. McNice's house.

I was honest, of course.

I said I had seen and heard SUSPICIOUS things.

And guess what? Alice told me off!

How can a spy tell off another spy for spying?

Well, Edison, I'll tell you how.

Eliza, would you spy on your friend Amy? Because Mrs. McNice is my friend, you know!

So I guess a family spy meeting is out. After all, if the Senior Spy (Alice) doesn't think Mrs. McNice is SUSPICIOUS, why should the Junior Spy (me)?

But I can hear that strange FIZZY-BUZZY sound right now.

Even with my big ears on, I still can't work out what is making the noise.

I'm going to try to sleep.

Most likely I'll just lie awake thinking about more things that could make that strange FIZZY-BUZZY sound.

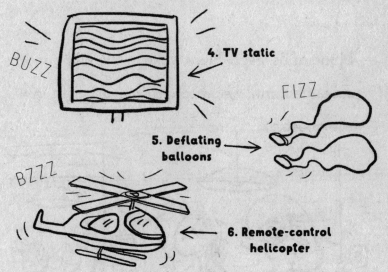

BUZZ

4. TV static

FIZZ

5. Deflating balloons

BZZZ

6. Remote-control helicopter

Yours fizzy-buzzingly,

Eliza Boom

The only spy in the house who feels SUSPICIOUS!

Thursday Morning
My Lab, 9 a.m.

Dear Edison,

None of us slept. Plum woke in the night and screamed until we switched on every light in the house.

WAAAAAH!!

I had to invent a soundproof bat cave to sleep in.

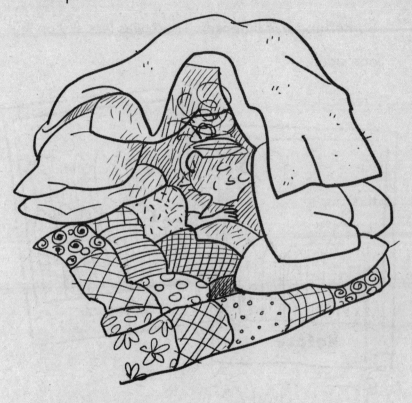

Poor Plum still misses her night light and everyone still blames Einstein. We need that night light!

So this morning I went outside to look for clues.

Something was different. There was less sky on one side!

Before

After

Mrs. McNice had used the huge planks of wood to make her fence taller.

I couldn't even see over it anymore!

We stayed out in the garden for a while. I tried to look for the night light AND more clues about Mrs. McNice, but I kept getting confused about what I was looking for. . . .

This could be a clue. For something. I'm just not sure WHAT!

The hardest part was that Einstein refused to walk on the grass. After what happened on Wednesday, he's terrified of ants.

When we came back inside, Alice said:

You've just missed Mrs. McNice. She popped in for coffee.

I couldn't believe I'd missed my chance to interrogate . . . um, I mean "politely ask" Mrs. McNice about the new fence. I inspected where she'd been for clues instead.

Exhibit A:
milk and two sugars

?

I was adding more to my Suspicious List . . .

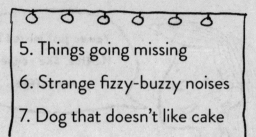

5. Things going missing

6. Strange fizzy-buzzy noises

7. Dog that doesn't like cake

. . . when clever Einstein found me another clue!

A REMOTE CONTROL
THAT I'D NEVER
SEEN BEFORE.

I've hidden the mystery remote control in my lab. I've also decided not to tell Alice or Dad about my list until I've got some PROOF.

Anyway, what if I'm still wrong about Mrs. McNice? I don't want Dad and Alice thinking I'm a terrible spy. I'll have to work solo.

Sometimes it's hard being an Assistant Inventor, a Junior Spy, AND a normal kid. For example, right now I'm off to gymnastics class. Spies need to be super fit and able to leap between buildings.

Yours cart-wheelingly,
Eliza Boom
Wheeeeeeeeee!!

Thursday Evening
My Lab, 6 p.m.

Dear Edison,

As we were leaving for gymnastics, I saw the
MOST SUSPICIOUS THING YET:

Mrs. McNice was throwing away the cupcakes
that Alice made for her!

I didn't tell Alice in case it
hurt her feelings.

But that has to be
SUSPICIOUS, doesn't
it? Perfectly yummy
cake in the trash!

Gymnastics class gave me a good idea for how to keep an eye on Mrs. McNice:

I needed to invent something to help me jump super high so I could see over that fence. I used the Super-Leg that Einstein didn't chew through to create . . .

... The Super-Leg Boing-Master!

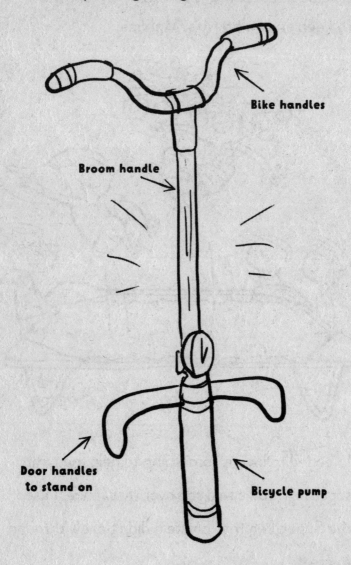

Bike handles

Broom handle

Door handles
to stand on

Bicycle pump

I've been practicing up here in my lab. It's great—I can touch the ceiling!

BOING!

BOING!

BOING!

ELIZA!

Uh-oh, Dad's calling me downstairs. I must have been boinging too much. Back soon!

Yours super-boingily,

Eliza

Thursday Night
My Lab, 8 p.m.

Dear Edison,

You won't believe it, but even more things have gone missing!

And guess who everyone STILL thinks is to blame?

Alice is missing her spy belt. It's got loads of great gadgets on it—like a micro earlight, a motion alarm, and a micro listener. Dad made it for her for their wedding anniversary last year.

Einstein would never take it! Would he??

And Dad is missing his spy pen. Not only does it write in invisible ink, but it can also make videos, record your voice, connect to the Internet, talk, AND even read your mood.

YOU ARE FEELING: INVENTIVE!

It was Dad's latest invention, and all his new ideas are stored on it.

But Einstein is INNOCENT. He wouldn't bury them. Those objects are just LOST in our house.

Dad says that losing that pen feels like losing

a piece of himself.

But which piece?

Brain?

Zombie Dad

Heart?

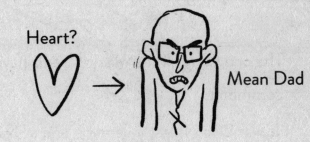

Mean Dad

Big toe??

Hopping Dad

It's time to think.

Edison, I've got it!

The one thing all the missing items have in common is:

night light   →

spy pen   →   METAL

spy belt   →

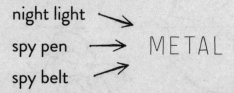

YES! All I need is a brilliant invention that uses
MAGNETS!

The trouble is, I need something from Dad's shed, but it's all locked up for the night.

Dad's shed

Oh, Edison, how will I sleep with this exciting idea fizzing around in my head?

Yours, fizz-buzzingly,

Eliza Boom

Junior Inventor with trusted (I think!)

sidekick, Einstein

Friday Morning
The Kitchen, 10 a.m.

Dear Edison,

I was up super early and snuck down to Dad's shed with Einstein.

But Dad was up early too, and I wasn't ready to tell him what I was working on. This called for some serious undercover work.

Luckily for me, Dad was working on his Virtual Reality Mask 2000.

He couldn't see us even when we were right in front of him!

I got what I needed from Dad's shed.

Before going back to the lab, I tested out
my Super-Leg Boing-Master to see over
Mrs. McNice's new fence.

But all I could see was Nancy. She was sitting very still in her usual position.

Hmm, Edison, I don't think Einstein and Nancy are a good match. Einstein is lively and fun. Nancy is like a statue!

After some super-high hopping, it was back to the lab.

Dad is always saying that recycling is important. So he'll probably be happy to find out that I've recycled his first-ever invention.

U-bend of a sink

Broom handle

Bag for storing bounty (treasure)

Compass

Frisbee that works as a metal detector (clever Dad!)

Boom's Bounty-Tracker

He made it when he was my age.

It was obvious that Dad had used a lot of things from around his house to make it. I bet Gran and Grandad had a few things to say about that!

That's why I knew Dad would understand why I HAD to use his Bounty-Tracker in my new invention. . . .

I have combined the main parts of Dad's Bounty-Tracker with my Echo-Detector to make . . . the Echo-Metal Bounty-Detector.

Let's call it the EMBD because it takes AGES to write its full name. With the hunting powers of my Echo-Detector plus the metal-tracking powers of Dad's Bounty-Tracker, I'll find those objects in the house in no time and prove Einstein's innocence!

Unfortunately, the accused dog, a.k.a. Einstein, didn't want to come—he'd been looking out of the window at Nancy since we got up.

So it was a solo mission to find Plum's night light, Dad's spy pen, and Alice's spy belt.

I went into every room in the house and piled up the things the EMBD found in my Secret Spy Stockroom (a.k.a. Plum's room), so that I wouldn't find the same thing twice.

Secret Spy Stockroom

This is what I ended up with:

THE GOOD NEWS:

The EMBD works! I found every single metal object in our house.

THE BAD NEWS:

I didn't find the spy belt, the spy pen, or the night light.

And now I've got to put all the stuff back.

I hope I can remember where everything goes!
Yours, still confused,
Eliza Boom
Assistant Inventor, Junior Spy, and about to be in big trouble if I don't clean up this mess!

Friday Night
My Lab, 8 p.m.

Dear Edison,

I'm going to confess something that I've never confessed before.

I've run out of ideas!

HELLOOOOOOO??

Don't tell ANYONE.

I've been walking around the house all afternoon pressing the buttons on this mysterious remote control that Einstein found yesterday.

It doesn't seem to do anything.

Alice and Dad have been up to say good night.

They said Nancy has been barking all day. Now that they mention it, I guess she has. . . .

I wonder if she's pining for Einstein the way he's pining for her.

I'm going to sleep with the remote control
under my pillow. Maybe then an idea will come
to me in my sleep about what it's actually for.

Bark

Yours, puzzled,

Eliza Boom

ONCE an Assistant Inventor and Junior Spy

who NEVER ran out of ideas . . .

P.S. I wish Nancy would stop barking so much!

Saturday Morning
The Garden, 9 a.m.

Dear Edison,

We didn't get much sleep AGAIN.

There was Plum screaming her head off because of the dark.

AND Nancy didn't stop barking all night!

Fizz

Bark

WAAAHHH!

Buzz

Bark

I got up to find Einstein guzzling
Lovey-Dovey-Doggy.

And that's when it struck me: all our problems

had begun the day Einstein met Nancy.

So it was time to retrace his steps.

I didn't know what I'd need for this mission, so I grabbed all the spy gear I could carry.

Plum wanted to come too. And Einstein was so excited about seeing Nancy again he forgot all about his fear of ants in the grass. That's real love.

We arrived at the spot where I'd first seen

Einstein squeezing under Mrs. McNice's fence.

I started to dig. Einstein kept watch.

Suddenly I hit something hard and my EMDB started going crazy. It had to be something metal. And soon I had uncovered . . .

PLUM'S NIGHT LIGHT!

Plum was so happy, she hugged it and toddled off into the house to show Alice.

Awww

So naughty Einstein DID take the night light after all.

But the spy belt and spy pen were STILL nowhere to be seen.

That's when I hit something else ... AN IDEA. What if there were TWO thieves at work?

If Einstein liked to take things and bury them, maybe Nancy did too!

First I tried boinging over the fence.

That didn't work.

Then I tried digging under the fence.

That didn't work either.

Finally, I decided to go
THROUGH the fence!

Okay—THAT
didn't work either.

Edison, there's only one thing to do: we'll have
to ring Mrs. McNice's doorbell and use clever
spy tactics. WATCH THIS SPACE.

Yours intrepidly,
Eliza Boom (with a bruised bottom)

Saturday Night
My Lab, 8 p.m.

Dear Edison,

You won't believe what's happened. I can still feel the shock fizzing in my veins!

Before heading over to Mrs. McNice's house, I decided to drop my EMDB and the Super-Leg Boing-Master back at our house. As Einstein and I were leaving, I saw Plum playing with that strange remote control. I decided to take it with me.

Nancy was barking like mad AGAIN. Was she trying to tell us something? Dogs on TV are always doing that.

I rang Mrs. McNice's doorbell and quickly hid.

Einstein played his part perfectly.

First he sat there. Then . . . he stayed sitting there. Then . . . he sat a bit more.

Then he picked up Mrs. McNice's door mat
and she chased him down the street!

I slipped inside the house. I had to work fast. . . .

Nancy was sitting on a very strange platform.
Up close, I could see there was something
wrong. Or rather, I could SNIFF it. Nancy
didn't smell like a dog, she smelled like . . . like
a new toy!

In surprise I dropped the remote control. And when it landed, Nancy barked!

So I picked it up and pressed one of the buttons. Every time I did, Nancy barked.

NANCY WAS A ROBOT DOG!

Suddenly, there was a noise behind me.

Mrs. McNice was back from chasing Einstein, and she didn't look like the kind lady who had brought us muffins anymore. She looked TRIPLE-SUSPICIOUS.

I tried to be super brave.

YOUR DOG IS A ROBOT, MRS. McNICE!

She didn't look one bit surprised. She looked
angry. She started a strange karate dance.

What are you doing here? Stand back! I am highly dangerous!

Just at that moment, Einstein came rushing in, trying to lick Mrs. McNice's face. He was protecting me, Edison! With doggy slobber. Good spy-dog!

Panicking, I pressed the remote control.
Nancy darted forward and sent Mrs. McNice
flying through the air! She landed —SPLAT—
against the wall.

She must have landed right on a switch, because a huge painting started to move completely BY ITSELF! Behind the painting was a SECRET ROOM that looked just like Alice's secret spy bunker.

Fizz

So many machines, all FIZZING and BUZZING away . . . and screens that all showed different rooms in OUR HOUSE.

Mrs. McNice had been spying! On US.

Buzz
Fzzz
Fizz
Bzzzz

Dad's → spy pen

Alice's spy belt

And then I saw Dad and Alice's missing things!

At that moment Mrs. McNice chased me out of the secret room. Thinking fast, I ran behind Nancy and kept pressing the buttons on the remote control, keeping Nancy as a guard dog between me and Mrs. McNice. Einstein was helping in his own way, licking her every time she tried to move.

Bark

Bark

Unfortunately, at the very moment Nancy ran

out of power . . .

. . . Mrs. McNice was COMING FOR ME!

NEWS FLASH:

even spies get scared.

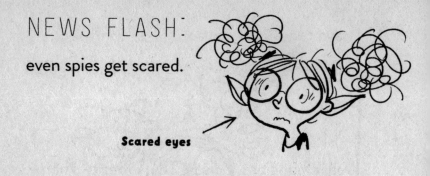

Scared eyes

Just when I thought I was in BIG TROUBLE,

and not even my inventions could save me . . .

a rescue squad arrived!

STAND BACK,
AGATHA CREEP!

They were all making a lot of noise.

I have to tell you, Edison, I was confused.
Why were they calling Mrs. McNice "Agatha
Creep"?

Well, I found out, Edison. That is her real name.
And she specializes in stealing enemy plans!

You see, this morning Alice had found my
SUSPICIOUS LIST.

It made her run a check on her digital spy files.
She found a match! Agatha Creep comes
from a rival spy family. She's been trying to
STEAL Dad's inventions. (And this time I bet
she wanted my inventions as well!)

Then Alice found five secret cameras hidden
around our house. That's what Mrs. McNice
must have been doing when she visited and went
upstairs "to the bathroom"!

After a spy conference, we decided not to call the police and to let Mrs. McNice/Agatha Creep go. On TWO conditions.

1. She never comes back again.

2. We get to keep Nancy. (Einstein will be pleased!)

Dad was relieved to have his spy pen back. One of the ideas he's stored on it is an invention for me!

Only I have to wait until tomorrow to find out what it is.

What a day! The Boom family is going to sleep well tonight, Edison, FOR A CHANGE!

Happy eyes

Yours, still FIZZING with excitement,
Eliza Boom
Excellent Junior Spy! (Alice and Dad both said so!)
And a really good inventor (they said that, too!)

Sunday Morning
My Lab, 10 a.m.

Dear Edison,

Six WONDERFUL things:

1. Dad's new invention was a special swimming backpack for me. It's made swimming totally nonsuspicious and extremely easy peasy.

2. Einstein and Nancy are best friends.

3. Plum has been sleeping soundly every night.

4. Alice's secret spy bunker is still secret. (Mrs. McNice never found it, phew!)

5. Amy and I made lots of Super-Leg Boing-Masters and sold them to our friends. Once we'd done our math . . .

... we had enough money left over to treat ourselves to lemonade!

And finally, wonderful thing number 6: Zoe Wakefield REALLY regrets not buying a Super-Leg Boing-Master.

Fizz-tastic!